Copper Finds a Scroll

by Amanda Hope Haley

Illustrated by Michelle Pitts

Learn more about
biblical archaeology
and hermenutics
when you read these books by
Amanda Hope Haley

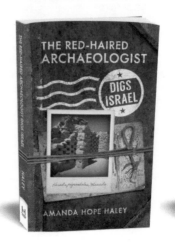
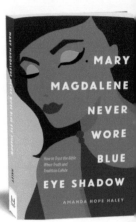

THE RED-HAIRED ARCHAEOLOGIST

presents

Copper Finds a Scroll

by Amanda Hope Haley

Illustrated by Michelle Pitts

Copper

is a hound dog.

Sometimes his
ears feel too long
and his **legs**
seem too short,

but they help him
to **track** and **dig**.

Copper's friend, Amanda, is an **archaeologist.**

She loves to dig too.

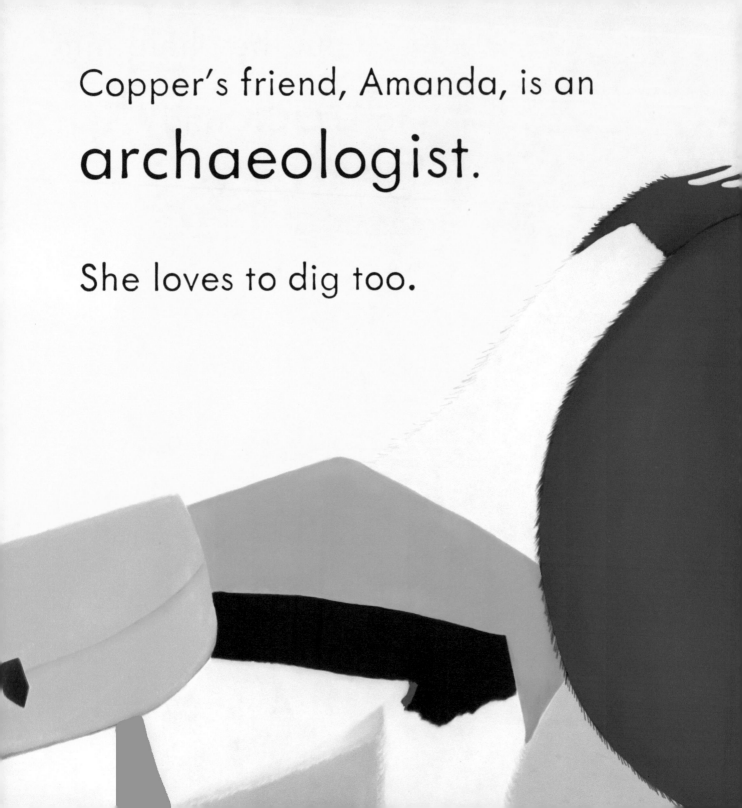

She takes
Copper
everywhere
she goes.

One day Copper was helping Amanda dig

next to the Dead Sea in Israel.

She was finding

jars and lamps and bones,

when Copper **smelled**
something else.

He
followed

his nose up the **sandbag stairs** ...

. . . along a windy **dirt trail,**

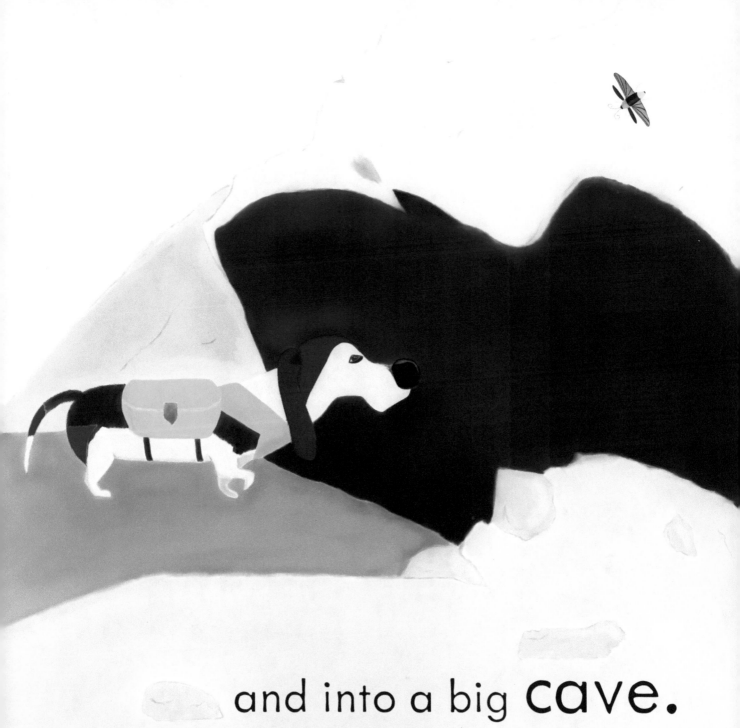

and into a big cave.

It was **dark** in the cave,
so Copper could not see.

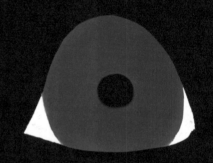

He did not like to be
alone in the dark.

Copper started to turn around . . .

. . . and tripped on his right ear.

"Ouch!"

he yelped.

A thousand fireflies awakened.

They **lit up** the cave,

and Copper saw a lot of jars...

. . . and an old hairy goat.

Mr. Goat was waking up from a nap, shaking his **head**, stretching his **neck**, and kicking his **legs**.

He knocked over one of the  big jars, and it broke.

Something rolled out.

"What are you doing in this **cave**?" asked Mr. Goat.

"No one has been here for almost **2,000 years!**"

Copper answered, "I was down in the valley with Amanda,

digging for old jars and lamps and bones,

when I smelled something else. I followed my nose into this cave."

"You have found an ancient library. A long time ago, scribes copied holy words onto scrolls.

They put the scrolls inside those jars,

hid them in this **cave,**

and asked my
family to **protect** them."

"I've heard that story before!

Right now, Amanda is in the valley **excavating** the city where those scribes lived.

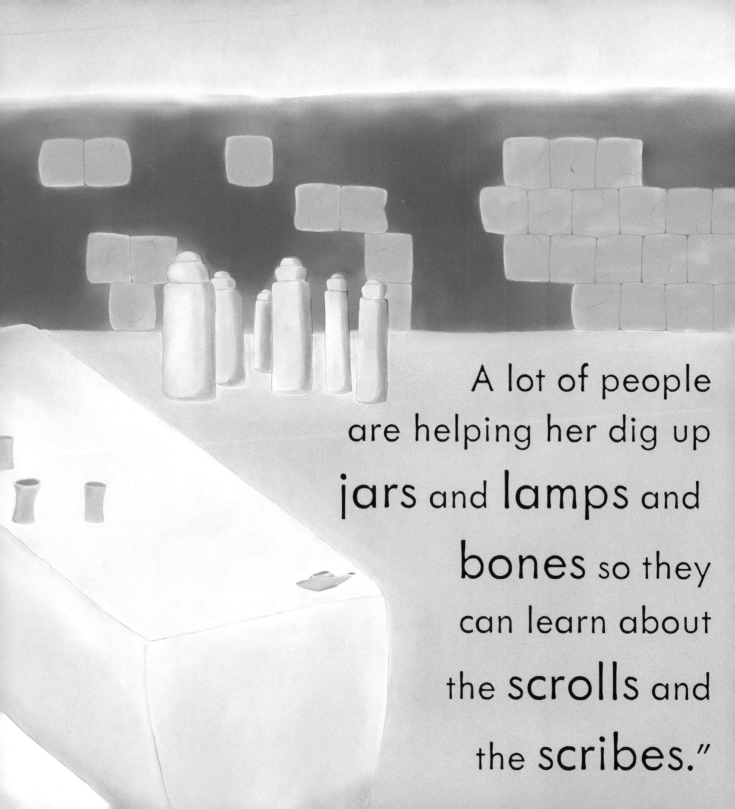

A lot of people are helping her dig up **jars** and **lamps** and **bones** so they can learn about the **scrolls** and the **scribes**."

"Those scribes loved the Bible, so a lot of the scrolls have words copied from the Old Testament. Take this Great Isaiah Scroll down to Amanda. It tells a very special story."

"Thank you, Mr. Goat.

I promise I'll protect it!"

Carrying the **scroll** in his pack—

here it wouldn't get damaged or dusty—

Copper put his **nose** to the ground
and followed the path back
down to Amanda at the
Dead Sea's coast.

It was late in the day,

and Amanda was calling Copper's name.

"Copper, I've told you never

to **wander** away from me!"

"I'm sorry I scared you,

but look at what I found!

Up in those **caves**, I met an old goat.

He takes care of a lot of **scrolls**,

but he wants you to **protect** this one."

Amanda sat down,

put on her white gloves,

and gently opened the scroll.

"A long, long time ago,

a prophet named Isaiah said

God would come here to be with us

This **scroll** contains that promise:

'a virgin shall conceive,
and bear a son,
and shall call his name
Immanuel.'"

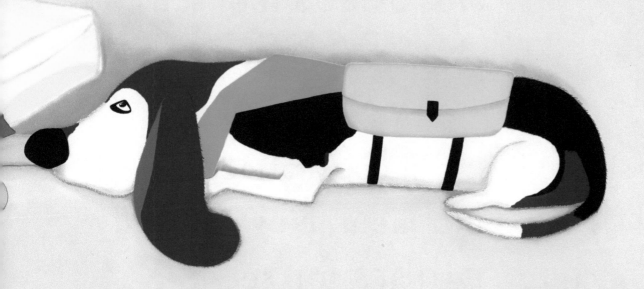

"Isaiah's prophecy was fulfilled 700 years after this promise, and not long before the scribes made this scroll."

Copper asked,
"Was Jesus that son Isaiah described?"

"Yes! You found a copy of Jesus's birth announcement. Now we will protect it so others can see it too!"

A PAGE FOR PARENTS!

Archaeology is the study of what our ancient ancestors left behind. It helps us learn how they lived and what they believed.

The Dead Sea is the lowest place on Earth. Its air is hot and salty, so perishable scrolls were preserved there for 2,000 years in clay jars.

Tradition says the Dead Sea Scrolls were first found by a goatherd in the caves at Qumran in 1947, as he was looking for a lost animal.

The scrolls were made of tanned animal skins called parchment that is heavy to carry but strong enough to be re-rolled many times.

The scribes were Essenes--a monastic community that spent their time copying sacred texts. They hid the Dead Sea Scrolls in the caves to protect them from the invading Roman army.

The Great Isaiah Scroll is the largest and best-preserved of the DSS. It contains almost all of the Book of Isaiah and was made in 125 BC. Isaiah 7:14 prophesied the Messiah would be born to a virgin.

For more information, visit the official website of the Dead Sea Scrolls:
https://www.deadseascrolls.org.il/home

Join Copper on his next adventure, when he

Finds a Manger

during Amanda's dig
in Bethlehem.

CPSIA information can be obtained
at www.ICGtesting.com
Printed in the USA
LVHW070742131021
700312LV00002B/70